P9-DEU-726

SUPERDUPER TEDDY

BY JOHANNA HURWITZ

The Adventures of Ali Baba Bernstein
Aldo Applesauce
Aldo Ice Cream
Baseball Fever
Busybody Nora
Class Clown
Class President
The Cold and Hot Winter
DeDe Takes Charge!
The Hot and Cold Summer
Hurray for Ali Baba Bernstein
Hurricane Elaine
The Law of Gravity
Much Ado About Aldo
New Neighbors for Nora
Nora and Mrs. Mind-Your-Own-Business
Once I Was a Plum Tree
The Rabbi's Girls
Rip-Roaring Russell
Russell and Elisa
Russell Rides Again
Russell Sprouts
Superduper Teddy
Teacher's Pet
Tough-Luck Karen
Yellow Blue Jay

SUPERDUPER TEDDY

by Johanna Hurwitz
illustrated by Lillian Hoban

MORROW JUNIOR BOOKS / NEW YORK

Inquiries should be addressed to
William Morrow and Company, Inc.,
105 Madison Avenue,
New York, NY 10016.
Printed in the United States of America.
1 2 3 4 5 6 7 8 9 10
Library of Congress Cataloging-in-Publication Data
Hurwitz, Johanna.
Superduper Teddy.
Summary: Encouraged by his gregarious sister and
his trusty Superman cape, five-year-old Teddy takes
his first steps toward independence.
[1. Brothers and sisters—Fiction. 2. City and
town life—Fiction. 3. Apartment houses—Fiction]
I. Hoban, Lillian, ill. II. Title.
PZ7.H9574Su 1990 [E] 89-13592
ISBN 0-688-09094-X
ISBN 0-688-09095-8 (lib. bdg.)

For a superduper person,
Caroline Feller Bauer

Contents

An Invitation for Teddy

Teddy lived in a medium-sized apartment building in New York City with his parents and his big sister, Nora. Nora was a real busybody, talking to strangers on the elevator, making new friends, and planning the games that she and Teddy would play. Teddy liked having a big sister. She had good ideas, and she taught him many things. Teddy was different from Nora. He was shy.

"That's just the way he is," said Mommy, shrugging her shoulders.

"He'll outgrow it," said Daddy.

"He's silly," said Nora. She wasn't shy at all.

Still, Nora was understanding and held Teddy's hand when they went visiting new people or when they went to the dentist's office for a checkup.

When he was with old friends like their neighbor Mrs. Wurmbrand, who was over eighty years old, or Russell, who lived on the second floor and was four years old, Teddy wasn't shy at all. Sometimes he even made so much noise and talked so much that everyone, including Teddy, forgot that he was ever the least bit shy.

When Teddy was only four years old, his mother had made him a Superman cape to wear on Halloween. Now, even though Teddy was five years old and it wasn't Halloween, he still liked to wear his cape around their apartment. Unlike pants, which became too short, or shoes, which became too tight, the cape still fit him fine.

Teddy liked to run through the hallway of the

apartment with the red cape flying behind him as he shouted, "S-U-P-E-R-M-A-N." Then he felt bigger and stronger and smarter than Nora, even if he wasn't. When they played pretending games, Teddy would often change them. So sometimes they played Snow White and Superman or Goldilocks and Superman. And even when they were playing checkers or sitting and listening to their father read a bedtime story, Teddy often liked to wear his cape. "It keeps me warm," he said.

One day Teddy came home from kindergarten holding an envelope that a boy named Bryan had given him. It was an invitation to a birthday party to be held on Saturday.

"I don't want to go," said Teddy.

"Oh, Teddy, of course you'll go," said his mother. "You don't want to hurt Bryan's feelings."

"It will hurt my feelings to go," Teddy explained.

Nora loved parties, and she had many invitations. There were twenty-five children in her second-grade class at school, and already, though it was only mid-October, she had been to four parties.

"Teddy, there will be cake and ice cream and games and prizes," she promised.

"I don't like games," said Teddy, who loved games at home but not away. "Especially pin-the-tail-on-the-donkey."

"You don't have to play anything you don't want to," said Mommy. "You can be an observer."

"Not if I don't go," observed Teddy. "I'm staying home."

When Saturday came, Teddy still didn't want to go to the party. Mommy took him to the store to buy a gift. They bought a set of dominoes because Mommy said, "Even if you don't go to the party, it will make Bryan sad not to get a present." She wrapped the box with paper that had cakes and candles and presents all over it.

"I'm staying home," said Teddy.

The party was at three o'clock. "Let's just take the present over to Bryan's house," said Mommy. "You don't have to stay."

"I'll stay home, and you can take it over," answered Teddy.

"We'll go together," said Mommy, taking Teddy's jacket out of the closet.

"I'm staying home," protested Teddy, as his mother zipped his jacket on him.

Teddy had never been to Bryan's house before. The invitation said he lived four blocks away, in an apartment building twice the size of Teddy's building.

At the entrance a doorman greeted them. He took one look at Teddy holding the wrapped gift and smiled. "Ah, you're going to the party."

"Yes," said Mommy. She smiled back.

Teddy said nothing, but he knew that he was not going to the party.

"It's in apartment fifteen K," said the doorman. "The elevator is on your left."

Mommy and Teddy entered the building and walked toward the elevator.

"Teddy," Mommy said, "we'll just give Bryan his present, and you can stay for a little while."

Teddy didn't answer, but he was determined not to stay.

On the fifteenth floor they had no trouble finding the apartment. Balloons were taped around the door, and there was a lot of noise coming from inside.

Mommy rang the bell, and the door was opened by a tall man.

"Happy birthday," said Mommy. "You must be the father of the birthday child."

"Yes, I am. Come in," the man said.

Mommy entered the apartment, pulling Teddy in with her. There were so many children that the room looked like a school.

"How many children are here?" Mommy asked in amazement. The parties for Nora and Teddy were usually limited to four or five friends.

"I think Ethel said thirty-five," the man answered. "It feels like a hundred."

"Well, Teddy," said Mommy, giving him a little push, "go and give your present to the birthday child."

HAPP
BIRTH
15 K

Teddy didn't budge.

"Don't be shy. Go and play with your friends," she encouraged him.

"No," said Teddy, standing his ground. "I don't know any of them. They are not my friends."

"Oh, Teddy," said Mommy, "of course you do. Go look for Bryan."

Suddenly a girl about the age and size of Nora came up to Teddy. "Who are you?" she asked.

"Teddy," whispered Teddy.

"What's in the package?"

"Dominoes," Teddy whispered.

"I already have three sets," she said, walking off in disgust.

"Tiffany!" said the man who had opened the door for Mommy and Teddy. "Be polite. We can return the duplicate gifts next week. Now greet your friend nicely."

"I don't know who he is, and I don't want any more dominoes," the girl called out.

The man turned to apologize. "I'm sorry. This

birthday business has gone to her head, and I hear that seven is a terrible age."

"The dominoes aren't for her," said Teddy. "They're for Bryan."

"Bryan? There's no Bryan here. At least I don't know him if he is here," said the man, looking around at all the children.

"But isn't this his birthday party?" asked Mommy.

"I told you I don't know anyone here," said Teddy.

Mommy fumbled in her coat pocket for the invitation. The date, the time, and the house were all the same. But the apartment number was different. The invitation said 5A.

"I'm so sorry," she mumbled, pulling Teddy by the hand. "We seem to be in the wrong apartment."

Teddy thought she seemed as eager to leave as she had been to come. They got off the elevator on the fifth floor. It was quiet at 5A, almost as if there were no party. A woman and a boy about Teddy's age opened the door together.

"Hi, Bryan," said Teddy.

"I hope we're not late," said Mommy, explaining about the mix-up and how they had gone to the wrong party.

"Teddy is the only other guest," Bryan's mother said, smiling. "We also invited another boy from school named Steven, but he has tonsillitis, and he couldn't come."

Teddy let go of his mother's hand. He walked into the apartment and handed Bryan the package wrapped in the special paper. "Where should I put my jacket?" he asked, as he opened the zipper unaided. Bryan took both the jacket and the gift. He put the first on his bed, and he opened the second.

"Oh, look," he called to his mother. "Dominoes, just like the ones we have at school."

Bryan and Teddy sat right down on the living-room floor and began to play together with the dominoes.

DOMINOES

Teddy's mother said good-bye to Teddy and Bryan and Bryan's mother. Teddy was so busy with Bryan he hardly noticed. The next hour and a half passed very quickly. When Mommy returned to pick him up, Teddy was happily eating ice cream and cake.

"I won a prize," he told his mother. "I got the booby prize for pinning the tail on the refrigerator door instead of on the donkey." His prize was a paddle with a little rubber ball attached to it.

"I told you parties are fun!" Nora said, when Teddy came home.

"Sometimes they are fun, and sometimes they aren't," said Teddy.

And he was right.

Grandpa Tells a Story

Two of Teddy's most favorite people in all the world were Grandma and Grandpa. So it was strange that he should be so unhappy when Mommy told him and Nora that their grandparents were coming to visit and were going to sleep over for two nights. He was unhappy because Mommy and Daddy would be away. They were going to Connecticut for the weekend to attend a wedding.

"Why can't we all go to the wedding?" asked Nora.

But the answer was no. An old friend of Daddy's was getting married, and the invitation did not include the children.

It was strange to wake up on Saturday morning and find Grandma in the kitchen fixing breakfast.

"What are you making?" asked Teddy, looking at the pot on the stove.

"Oatmeal," said Grandma.

"Oh, Grandma," explained Nora, "Mommy only uses that to make oatmeal cookies. We don't eat it in the morning."

"A hot cereal is very good for breakfast," said Grandma, stirring the contents of the pot.

"I don't want any," said Teddy.

"Why, Teddy! Your mother had a bowl of hot cereal every morning when she was your age.

Don't you want to grow up to be big and strong just like your mother?" asked Grandma.

"No," said Teddy. "I don't want to grow up to be a lady."

Grandma had to use a lot of coaxing and a lot of raisins and a lot of sugar to get Teddy and Nora to sample the oatmeal.

"I like oatmeal cookies better because they're crunchy," said Teddy. "Will Mommy be home by breakfast tomorrow?" he asked anxiously.

"No," said Grandma. "But tomorrow I'm going to make pancakes, and you can help. I always made pancakes for Sunday morning breakfast when your mother was a girl."

After breakfast they all went to the playground. Teddy played in the sandbox, and Nora went on the swings. It was just like any other Saturday morning except that Grandma and Grandpa were sitting on the park bench instead of Daddy.

Just before lunchtime, it began to get cloudy.

"It looks like rain," Grandma commented. "I think I'll fix some hot soup for lunch."

"I'd rather have a peanut-butter sandwich, please," said Nora politely.

"Me too," said Teddy, less politely.

So they had peanut butter. Grandma cut up some carrot sticks for the children, too.

"No, I don't want any," said Teddy. "I like cooked carrots better because they're soft."

By the time lunch was over it was raining outside. "How much longer until Mommy and Daddy come home?" asked Teddy.

"About twenty-four hours," answered Grandpa.

"That's too long," said Teddy. He was close to tears. "There's nothing to do."

"We could play a game of rummy," suggested Grandpa. He had taught Teddy and Nora how to play the last time he had come for a visit.

"I don't feel like it," said Teddy.

"Shall we all work together to make your giant jigsaw puzzle? The one that has a hundred pieces," suggested Grandma.

"I don't feel like it," said Nora.

"Would you like to paint?"

"I don't feel like it," said Teddy.

"Perhaps there is something good on the television," said Grandpa, turning on the set. On the first channel there was a movie that didn't look very interesting, and men and women were talking together about boring things on the other channels. Nothing seemed right for a boy of five and a girl of seven, and Grandpa turned off the set.

"I wish we could go to a wedding," said Nora. "That's what I feel like doing."

"Yes," said Teddy in agreement. "I feel like going to a wedding too."

"Come, let's sit on the sofa together," said Grandpa to the children. "Did I ever tell you about the wedding that I once went to?"

"Tell us about it, Grandpa," said Nora.

"There used to be three sisters living across the street from me when I was a boy," began their grandfather. "When they first moved into the empty house across the street, I went over and asked if they would like to play with me. Their mother explained that one sister had a lot of chores to do, but the other two could come out. So we played hide-and-seek. But those girls, Annabella and Lulubella, cheated every minute. I didn't like them at all. So after that I didn't play with them very often. But one day my parents had to go on a trip, and they didn't want to leave me alone. So they asked our neighbors across the street if I could stay with them."

"Couldn't your grandparents come and stay with you?" asked Nora.

"They lived too far away," explained Grandpa. "So early in the morning, even before breakfast," he continued, "I went across the street. The mother and the two sisters were just sitting down to eat scrambled eggs and toast and jelly and cocoa. It all looked delicious. They asked me to sit down. 'Where will your other sister sit?' I asked Annabella."

Grandpa paused. "Do you know what she said?" he asked.

The children shook their heads.

"She said, 'She has a special place of her own.' And I looked and saw she was sitting by the chimney corner and her breakfast was just some old crusts of bread."

"It was Cinderella!" gasped Teddy and Nora at the same time.

"Why, yes," said Grandpa. "How did you know her name? I hid some toast under my napkin, and after breakfast I gave it to her. Even though she was covered with ashes and cinders, she was very beautiful. Annabella and Lulubella were too busy to play that morning. Their mother took them to Macy's to buy fancy gowns for a big party that they had been invited to. Cinderella told me all about it. She wanted to go too, but she didn't have any pretty dresses. I helped her do all her chores and promised her that I would teach her how to play Parcheesi in the evening while the others were at the party."

"But you didn't," guessed Teddy.

"Well," said Grandpa. "In the evening, Annabella and Lulubella went off with their mother.

They looked ridiculous, and I knew that no one would want to dance with them. Cinderella was feeling much better about staying home since I was going to be with her, and we had just begun a game of Parcheesi. She had the red pieces and I had the green. Suddenly who should appear out of nowhere but—"

"Her fairy godmother!" shouted Teddy.

"Right," said Grandpa. "The fairy godmother said she would help Cinderella go to the ball.

" 'No thanks,' Cinderella answered. 'I want to stay home and play Parcheesi. We just began, but I'm winning already.'

" 'No, no,' the fairy godmother said. 'It's important that you go so that the handsome young prince can fall in love with you.'

"Well, Cinderella really didn't want to leave me, but she understood her duty. I helped her pick out a pumpkin and the rats and mice that the fairy godmother requested."

"Did you really see them all change into a coach and horses?" asked Teddy.

"Yes," said Grandpa. "It was better than any television show."

"And then what happened?" asked Nora.

"Well, Cinderella rode away, so I invited the fairy godmother to play Parcheesi with me instead. She had nothing else to do that evening, so she agreed. We played for hours and hours, and the nicest thing was that sometimes I won and sometimes she won. She played fair and didn't use her magic wand.

"Suddenly the clock struck twelve. 'I told Cinderella to get home and get a good night's sleep,' the fairy godmother complained. 'After all, she is still a growing girl.' She waved her wand, and everything was transformed back to the way it had been before."

"Except the glass slippers," interrupted Teddy.

"Right," said Grandpa. "Cinderella showed me the one she still had the next morning. It was as tiny and as delicate as could be, especially compared to my sneakers. Before long the prince came up and down the street ringing doorbells.

He was looking for the one who could fit the slipper that he had found. When he came to my house, I told him to save time and go directly to Cinderella."

"And he did, and they got married," said Nora.

"Right," said Grandpa. "And I went to the wedding."

"And they lived happily ever after," concluded Teddy.

"Yes," said Grandpa. "And Cinderella and the prince played Parcheesi with each other. But the two mean stepsisters were always unhappy, because they always cheated whenever they played."

"Oh, Grandpa," said Teddy, "you had funny neighbors when you were a boy."

"Yes," agreed Grandpa. "And now who wants to play a game of Parcheesi with me?"

So all afternoon, while it rained outside, they took turns playing Parcheesi, and no one cheated. After a while, Grandma went into the kitchen to start making supper. She remembered that Teddy liked some things crunchy and some things soft.

So she fixed one of each, fried chicken and mashed potatoes. Both Teddy and Nora said supper was delicious, and they ate every bite.

And the next morning they didn't have oatmeal.

And Mommy and Daddy came home very soon after.

Teddy Gets a Job

Mommy was helping Nora pack a small suitcase. She was going to have a sleep-over visit with her friend Sharon for *two* nights. It was the first time that she would be away for so long. Teddy watched her with admiration. He wished that he was as grown up as Nora, but he didn't want to have to sleep in another house for two nights to prove it. Now that he was in kindergarten, everyone said he was a big boy. But whatever he did, Nora had already done it before. He wished that just once he could do something that Nora had never done.

Nora was deciding whether she should pack her red polo shirt with blue stripes or her blue polo shirt with red stripes when the doorbell rang. Nora threw both shirts on her bed and ran with her mother to open the door. Teddy followed behind. It was always interesting when the doorbell rang.

At the door stood their across-the-hall neighbor, Anita. "Hi!" she greeted them all. "I've come to ask a favor. Actually, I want to offer Nora a job."

"A job? A job for me? Will I get money?" asked Nora with delight.

"Of course you'll get paid, if your mother agrees," said Anita. "Because of the holiday weekend, I'm going to be away for two nights. And I wondered if you would be able to feed Cassandra and give her fresh water while I'm gone."

"Oh, yes!" shouted Nora. Cassandra was the large, white cat that Anita had acquired a few months before. Both children adored the animal and wished that she belonged to them.

"Nora, you won't be home," Mommy reminded her. "You will be at Sharon's all weekend."

"Oh, no!" said Nora, stamping her foot with anger. Two minutes ago she had been happy about going to Sharon's, and now she was sorry.

"That's too bad," said Anita. "I guess I'll ask Eugene Spencer if he would like the job." Eugene had recently moved to the fourth floor, and he was eight years old.

"Eugene Spencer has a sore throat and a temperature," said Nora.

"I could do it," offered Teddy.

"What a good idea!" said Anita. "Cassandra knows and trusts you. All you have to do is open a fresh can of cat food tomorrow morning and another one on Sunday."

"You can't work can openers, Teddy," said Nora.

Teddy thought for a minute. "You could open

the cans and leave them inside the refrigerator," he said to Anita. "I can open a refrigerator."

"How will you get inside the apartment?" asked Nora.

"Oh, I'll leave my key, of course," said Anita.

"You don't know how to open doors with keys," Nora reminded Teddy.

"I'll open the door for him," said their mother, "as long as I don't have to go inside." Mommy was allergic to cats. They made her eyes get red and tear, and they made her sneeze, too.

So it was arranged, and Teddy had a job. He could hardly wait to give Cassandra her first meal. He wanted to go the minute that he woke up in the morning, but Mommy said that first he had to eat his own breakfast and that he had to put his clothes on, too.

"Cassandra is hungry," said Teddy. But he quickly dressed and, as usual, put on his Superman cape.

Mommy opened Anita's door for Teddy. He went inside. Cassandra had heard the sound of the key in the lock, and she stood in the hallway rubbing herself against Teddy's legs. He closed the door behind him and went into the kitchen. It felt strange to be in Anita's apartment without Anita. Teddy was glad that he was wearing his cape. It made him feel strong and brave, even if there wasn't anything to be afraid of. Teddy stood on tiptoe and turned on the kitchen-light switch. He felt better now that there was more light. Cassandra kept meowing, so Teddy hurried to open the refrigerator. Sure enough, right in front were the two cans of cat food waiting to be served. Teddy put one can on the floor for Cassandra and picked up her water bowl. It was almost empty. Since he couldn't reach the faucets at the sink, he pushed a chair over and climbed up on it. He filled the bowl with cold water and climbed down. As he did so, he tipped the bowl and water spilled all over the floor. Teddy looked for something he could use to wipe it up. There was a paper-towel roller, but there were no towels on it. He looked in the sink for a sponge. There was nothing. It wouldn't be nice to leave puddles of water on the floor, thought Teddy. He wiped his wet hands on his cape and then decided that he should take it off and use it as a towel. Cassandra didn't pay any attention to Teddy as he mopped up the water. She was too busy eating her tuna fish.

Then Teddy noticed for the first time that there was a faint buzzing sound in the apartment. It had a steady ring, and it just kept on and on. It wasn't the doorbell. Teddy knew what that sounded like. It wasn't the telephone. Teddy listened hard, trying to figure out what the sound was. Maybe there was a burglar in Anita's bedroom, and he was ringing a bell to make Teddy go away. Teddy began to feel afraid. He was going to rush back to the safety of his own apartment when a thought occurred to him. Maybe the burglar would kidnap Cassandra. Quietly, so the burglar wouldn't hear him, Teddy walked toward the direction of the ringing, which was coming from Anita's bedroom. Teddy pushed the

UTTER
MEOW
FRUIT

door open. The room was rather dark and he couldn't see too well, but the ringing was much louder.

"You can't steal Cassandra," he shouted into the room.

There was no answer.

He walked inside the room and turned on the light. There on the table by Anita's bed was her alarm clock, and it was ringing. Anita must have forgotten and put the switch on. Teddy went over to the clock and figured out how to turn off the sound. Then he turned off the light in the bedroom and returned to the kitchen.

"It's all right, Cassandra. You're safe," he reassured the cat. She didn't seem worried at all. She just went on eating.

Teddy finished mopping up the water and refilled the cat's water bowl again. This time he managed to put it on the floor without spilling it.

"Good-bye Cassandra. Don't be lonely. I'll be back tomorrow," said Teddy. He was glad that his mother didn't give him food just once a day.

He took his wet cape and returned to his own apartment. "It's a good thing that I had this with me," he told his mother. "It came in very handy. Superman only uses his cape for flying, but I had to use mine for drying. There weren't any towels in Anita's kitchen, so I used my cape instead."

"Good thinking!" said Teddy's mother. She put the cape into the laundry hamper, and Teddy went downstairs to the second floor to play with Russell.

The next morning, when Teddy went to Anita's apartment, he couldn't wear his cape because it was still in the laundry. Cassandra once again greeted him at the door. Teddy bent down and stroked the cat's white fur. "Soon Anita will be home," he said to the animal. "She'll be glad to see you again." Then Teddy noticed something that he hadn't seen the day before. There was a trail of dirt on the floor and muddy pawprints on the kitchen linoleum.

"Cassandra, what have you been doing?" asked Teddy. He followed the trail of prints and discovered that the cat had knocked down a flowerpot that had been on the kitchen windowsill.

"Oh, Cassandra, you were a bad cat!" scolded Teddy, as he righted the pot and tried to put some of the scattered soil back into it. He hoped that the plant inside wouldn't die. Teddy looked around for another location for the flowerpot. He was afraid that the cat would knock it over again, if he put it back on the sill. Teddy climbed onto a chair and reached a shelf above the sink. He put the plant there. "Don't look, Cassandra," he said. He didn't want the cat to jump from the chair to the shelf and topple the plant again.

When Teddy got down, he tried to clean up the rest of the dirt that was on the floor. He didn't want Anita to come home to a messy apartment. Maybe she wouldn't pay him if she saw the dirt all over the floor. Teddy did the best he could. There were no paper towels, and today he didn't have his cape. He looked around for something to clean the floor. He couldn't see anything in the kitchen that he could use. Then he got an idea.

He took off his sneakers and used his socks to wipe up the dirt on the floor. It was funny to be walking around in Anita's kitchen in his bare feet. Cassandra began to meow.

"Oh, Cassandra, I forgot your food," said Teddy. He went to the refrigerator and removed the can that was waiting inside. He put the empty can from the day before into Anita's garbage pail. He shook some of the dirt from his socks into the pail, too. Then Teddy refilled the cat's bowl with fresh water, taking care not to spill any. Cassandra seemed very happy now, so Teddy said good-bye and went home.

"Teddy! What's the matter with your feet?" asked his mother, when he walked barefoot into their apartment, holding his sneakers and socks in his hands. "I didn't have my cape, so I had to use my socks," said Teddy.

"Thank goodness Anita will be home tonight," said Mommy. "Every time you feed her cat you come home minus some clothing. One more trip

to her apartment and you'll be down to your underwear!"

When Anita returned home that evening, she rang the doorbell and presented Teddy with a dollar bill.

"You did a fine job taking care of Cassandra," she told Teddy. "You are a super cat sitter."

"What are you going to do with your money?" Nora asked.

"I'll put it in my bank and save it," he said. He was proud of his dollar bill, but he was even prouder of something else. He had earned money, and Nora had never done that. For the first time Teddy had done something first, before Nora. That made having a job even more special.

Squabbling

Some days begin badly.

There was only one portion of cereal left in the box, and Teddy grabbed it for his breakfast.

"That's not fair," said Nora, and to prove it she gave Teddy a pinch. Teddy jumped and spilled his glass of orange juice on Nora's red slacks.

Teddy laughed. "You look like you wet your

OAT
CRUNCH

pants. You're a baby, like Russell's sister, Elisa."

"I am not," said Nora. "It was your fault."

"Stop squabbling," said Mommy. "Nora, put those pants in the laundry and get the green ones out of your drawer. And hurry. You don't want to be late for school," she added, as she wiped up the juice from the floor.

"I don't like the green slacks," complained Nora. "They're itchy. This is going to be a very bad day. And it's all Teddy's fault."

Now Teddy felt that Nora wasn't being fair. Later in kindergarten, though, he became so busy, building with the blocks and painting at the easel and learning a new song and eating cookies, that he forgot that Nora was angry at him.

But after school Teddy could see that Nora was still angry. She didn't like the cookies Mommy offered them for their after-school snack. "At least, I wish we had chocolate milk," she complained. Then they went with their mother to the supermarket to pick up a few groceries. Mike, who worked in the store, was stamping the price on the soup cans when they walked down the aisle. He was an old friend of theirs.

"Here," he said, holding out the stamping device. "Give me your hands."

The game was an old one that had begun a long time ago. He would put a price on the back of their hands. Mike stamped a number on Nora's hand. It said 29¢ in blue ink. Then he adjusted the device before he touched it to Teddy's skin. Nora looked at the back of Teddy's hand. It said 92¢.

"Teddy is *not* worth more than me," she said angrily.

"They are both the same," said Teddy, looking at the 2 and the 9 on both their hands.

"Hush," whispered Mommy. "It isn't important."

"Yes, it is!" said Nora, and she gave Teddy a kick.

Teddy didn't know much about arithmetic yet, but he knew all about punches, pinches, pokes, and kicks. Mommy separated the children and pulled them to the check-out line.

"Really," she said, "if you act like animals, I will have to put you both in cages. Separately," she added.

Back at home, Nora decided to read her new library book. Teddy couldn't read yet, so he started to nag his sister.

"Read to me," he begged.

"No. Leave me alone," said Nora. She was reading about Betsy, who was lucky. She didn't have a brother who spilled juice on her clothes or bothered her when she was reading.

Teddy leaned over Nora's shoulder.

"Go away," said Nora, pushing him.

"It's my room, too. I can stay here."

"This is my bed. Get off."

From the kitchen their mother called out. "It's four thirty!" It was time for the children's television program.

"Let's not watch that old show," said Nora, when they went to the living room. "I want to

see the program that my friend Sharon watches today."

"No," shouted Teddy, butting his head into Nora's stomach.

Nora hit out at Teddy. He began to cry, but at the same time he wrestled her away from the TV set. "I'll make mince squeaks out of you," he shouted.

"What's going on here?" asked Mommy running into the living room. "Stop this squabbling!"

"Nora started it," said Teddy.

"It's Teddy's fault," said Nora. And they began to fight again.

Mommy turned off the TV set. "No TV today. Now go to your room this instant."

Both Teddy and Nora were in tears. Neither they nor their mother knew if they were crying because of their wounds or the loss of television privileges.

"If we had two television sets like Sharon, then we could both watch what we want," whined Nora.

"Never mind," said Mommy, "then you two would find something else to fight about instead."

Nora stopped crying first after their mother went into the kitchen. "Do you want to play something?" she asked Teddy.

"Aren't you angry anymore?" he asked, wiping away his tears.

"It's no fun," said Nora. "Let's play Little Red Riding Hood. Do you want to be the wolf?" she offered.

"No," said Teddy. "I want to be the woodcutter who rescues Little Red Riding Hood."

"I know," said Nora. "My doll can be Little Red Riding Hood, and I will be the wolf."

They began to play. Nora spoke in different tones to say, "Grandmother, what big eyes you have!" since her doll couldn't talk. Then she answered in a gruff voice, "All the better to see you with, my dear." Nora and Teddy often acted out stories. It was a lot of fun. Soon the wolf gobbled up Little Red Riding Hood, but then Teddy the woodcutter appeared on the scene.

"You awful creature," he shouted at Nora the wolf. "I am going to kill you."

Just as he was saying those words, the bedroom door opened and Mommy and Daddy walked into the room.

"Grrrr," said Nora. "I will bite you with my sharp teeth."

"Stop it! Stop it!" shouted Mommy. "You have been fighting all day long. It's no wonder that I have such a dreadful headache from it all."

"What are you fighting about?" asked their father.

"We're not fighting," said Teddy with surprise.

"We're just playing a game," said Nora. "What's for supper?" she asked.

"Meatballs and spaghetti," said Mommy.

"Super!" said Teddy. "I bet if the wolf had meatballs and spaghetti for supper, he would never have eaten Little Red Riding Hood."

Some days finish up fine.

A Superduper Pet

For as long as Teddy and Nora could remember, they had been longing for a pet. "Couldn't we have a dog?" Nora begged her parents, whenever she saw someone walking a dog on the street.

"It isn't fair for a dog to live in a small city apartment," their father repeated over and over again.

"I wish we could have a cat," Nora said, whenever they saw Anita's white, furry Cassandra or whenever they saw a stray cat walking in the street.

"You know I'm allergic to cats," her mother said.

"I wish we could have an alligator," said Teddy. It had been his choice for years, ever since he had first seen one at the zoo. No one ever said that it wasn't fair to keep an alligator in an apartment. And no one in the family was allergic to alligators, as far as they knew. But, of course, they never got an alligator. One year their grandmother gave Teddy a lovely stuffed toy alligator, but it didn't count. He also had many teddy bears, and Nora had a large toy rabbit.

Stuffed animals were useful in some of their games of make-believe, and they could cuddle with them when they went to sleep. But still, both Teddy and Nora wished for a real live pet of their own.

A cousin of Nora's friend Sharon had a cat that gave birth to six kittens. Sharon's mother agreed that her daughter could have one, and Sharon

ETS

told Nora that if she wanted one she could get it for her. Kittens are so tiny that Nora didn't see how her mother's eyes and nose would even know the difference when it was in the house. "Kittens grow big very quickly," said Mommy, "and besides, my nose is very smart."

Then their new neighbor, Eugene Spencer, told them that he was getting a dog for his next birthday. "I'll let you have a turn walking him," he generously offered Nora and Teddy, when they expressed their envy.

Not everyone they knew had a pet. Russell didn't. He only had a baby sister, Elisa. Their old friend Mrs. Wurmbrand didn't have a pet. Mrs. Ellsworth, a neighbor who believed that people should mind their own business, didn't have a pet either.

"Why would anyone want to have a dog or a cat? They eat too much and they make a mess," she said, when Nora and Teddy told her the news about Eugene Spencer's good luck. Too late the children remembered, as their mother stood talking and agreeing with her, that Mrs. Ellsworth never did practice what she preached and mind her own business.

Apparently, Teddy and Nora would never have a pet of their own.

"How would you like us to get a tank with some fish?" their father offered.

"I don't want fish. They're too wet," said Nora.

"I want a pet we can touch," said Teddy.

"Could we get a gerbil?" asked Nora. But a gerbil was also out of the question. Nora had once brought home the class gerbils for a holiday week, and Mommy had sneezed all week long.

"Any animal with hair is impossible," she said.

"I have hair. How come I don't make you sneeze?" asked Teddy.

Mommy laughed. "I have hair too," she said. "Luckily, I'm not allergic to myself."

Then Teddy said, "Alligators don't have any hair."

But, of course, an alligator was also impossible.

"Even if there are alligators for sale in New York City pet shops, they grow to be eight feet long and they need to eat lots and lots of fish," Daddy reminded Teddy.

"Someday perhaps we'll find a small, bald animal that isn't wet and doesn't eat a lot of food," he said.

"And doesn't make a lot of noise," their mother added.

"I don't think there is such an animal," said Nora with disgust.

Teddy refused to give up. He kept thinking about pets. Whenever he walked to the post office with his mother and they passed the pet shop, Teddy always insisted that they stop and look in the window. They usually went in the afternoon, when Teddy had finished with kindergarten but Nora was still in school. Teddy was sure that one day he would find the perfect pet and they would bring it home and surprise Nora and Daddy. Once there was a mother rabbit with eight darling little bunnies in the pet-shop window. Another time there were puppies. One day there were several large parrots.

"Do feathers make you sneeze?" Teddy asked his mother. The parrots had bright green feathers, and when they went inside the store to look at them more closely, they could hear that one had even learned to say, "Hello."

But they were much too expensive, and Mommy said that their loud squawks would give her a headache.

While they were inside the store looking at the parrots, Teddy noticed an animal he had never seen there before. It was a turtle. Not a tiny little one that lives in a bowl of water, but a much bigger turtle, the size of Mommy's shoe. It was walking about in a large tank and chewing on a leaf of lettuce.

"Mommy!" shrieked Teddy. "I found the perfect pet for us."

Teddy's mother turned to look. "That is a tortoise," the shopkeeper told them.

"Can we buy him?" Teddy begged. Before Mommy could say anything, she began to sneeze. The animal smells in the shop were irritating her nose. "How much does it cost?" she asked, while she blew her nose.

The price was so much less than the cost of the parrots that it seemed very cheap. Of course, Mommy forgot to include the price of the glass tank or the taxi fare home. She also forgot to go to the post office and buy her stamps. But Teddy was so delighted that the money seemed well spent.

Teddy could hardly wait till Nora came home from school. He ran from the tortoise to the kitchen clock a dozen times, waiting for the hands to show three thirty, which was the time Nora would be home. Tortoises are supposed to move very slowly, but this tortoise moved much faster than the hands on the clock.

At last she arrived.

"Nora, we have a pet! Guess what it is," he shouted, as she walked in the door.

"Where is it?" demanded Nora, looking about. "Is it a dog like Eugene Spencer's?"

"No," said Teddy.

"Mommy, did you get some medicine so you won't be allergic to cats?" asked Nora.

"No," said their mother.

"It's in our bedroom," said Teddy, who couldn't wait any longer as Nora looked under the living-room sofa and in the corners of the wrong rooms, searching for the new pet.

"A giant turtle!" Nora shrieked, when she saw the animal. "What shall we name her?"

"I think it's only fair to let Teddy pick out a name, since he was the one to find the creature that meets all our requirements," said Mommy.

"His name is Mr. Hush," said Teddy, "because he is so quiet."

"How do you know it's a *he*?" asked Nora.

"I just know," said Teddy, and since nobody in the family could prove him wrong, the tortoise remained Mr. Hush.

Mr. Hush spent almost as much time out of his

tank as inside. He walked about the apartment looking over his new home. He seemed to approve and enjoy his first dinner of cucumber and apple. He let the children hold him, and he didn't try to jump out of their arms or scratch them as Sharon's kitten did.

He was clean. He didn't eat too much. He didn't shed hairs. And his name fitted. He didn't make any noise at all.

Everyone agreed that he was a superduper pet.

"Teddy, you were smart to find him," said Nora.

Teddy smiled. He was feeling superduper too.

Teddy Entertains

When it was Halloween, Nora planned a party. Seven classmates wearing costumes came to eat and play together. Of course she had a birthday party, and when Valentine's Day came, she arranged another party for her friends. "Nora is a born hostess," observed Mommy, who usually made the cookies and bought decorated napkins for these events.

In time, Teddy would have a birthday party too, but his birthday was still a long way off. "Teddy, you should plan more parties," said Nora. "They're lots of fun."

Teddy thought about it. But he was still shy. He preferred to invite one friend at a time. He liked to have his school friend Bryan come to play, and he liked to have Russell come to play. But he worried when he had two friends together. Sometimes they could not agree on a game or which role to assume. So Teddy didn't think he would plan any parties after all.

One Friday morning, in early March, the weather was especially lovely. The smell of spring was in the air. Teddy's kindergarten teacher, Linda, decided the morning was too nice to stay indoors. It was a perfect day for them all to take a walk in the neighborhood. Several children and the assistant teacher were absent with chicken pox. Teddy had already had chicken pox the year before.

Linda helped the twelve healthy children put

their jackets back on, and they all paraded out of the school building and down the street. First they stopped in front of Jerry's Fine Fruits and admired all the vegetables and fruits that were displayed. Teddy saw some tiny oranges, small enough to make juice for a mouse.

"Look at the oranges," he said pointing them out to Linda.

"Those aren't oranges," she told him. "They are kumquats."

"Kumquats, kumquats," Teddy repeated to himself. He loved new words.

Jerry came out of his shop to greet the children. "Good morning," he said to them, his moustache turning up as he smiled.

"Do you like my fruit?" Jerry asked. "Tell your mothers to come and buy. I have many specials today."

"I like the baby oranges," said Arthur loudly. He hadn't heard Linda tell Teddy what those little fruits really were.

"Those aren't oranges; they're kumquats," Teddy called out, full of his new knowledge.

"Good for you," said Jerry, and he reached into the pile of fruit and handed one to Teddy. Looking at it more closely, Teddy could see that although the color was exactly like an orange's, the shape was different. It was more like a tiny egg than a round orange.

He started to hand the fruit back to the store owner, but Jerry stopped him. "You may keep it."

Teddy glowed. Wouldn't Nora and his parents be surprised when he brought this special fruit home?

The class said good-bye to Jerry and continued on their walk. They passed the shoe store and the Laundromat. When they passed the bakery, the smell of freshly baked cakes and cookies and bread filled the air.

"I'm hungry," called out Emily.

"Me too," echoed several of the other children.

"Just one more block, and we will turn back

to school and have our juice and cookies," said Linda.

Suddenly Teddy had an idea. He couldn't wait to show off his newly acquired kumquat. "That's my house," he said, pointing to the brick building on the next corner. "We could have juice and cookies there."

"Teddy, your mother isn't expecting us," said Linda. "Perhaps we can go another day."

"My mother likes company," insisted Teddy. "We can ring the downstairs bell and tell her."

In the lobby of the apartment house where Teddy lived, there was a special telephone that enabled visitors to call up to the apartment they were going to visit. The whole class pushed into the lobby while Linda pushed the intercom button.

"Yes?" called back a faint voice. It was Mommy.

"This is Linda with Teddy's class. He has invited us to visit. Is it all right with you if we come up?"

There was a pause. "What?" asked Mommy,

sounding surprised. Linda repeated her question, and Teddy called into the mouthpiece of the phone, "Mommy, you said I could have my friends over whenever I wanted."

"Yes," agreed Mommy. "Come on up."

Henry the doorman watched as Linda and the twelve children stood waiting for the elevator.

"Teddy, what do you think you're doing? You're acting just like Nora," Henry said, laughing. He was used to Nora and her social ways, but Teddy wasn't acting in his usual style today.

The elevator came and everyone pushed inside.

"Maybe you should go up in two shifts," said Henry.

"I have to watch all the children," explained Linda. "It's better if we all stay together."

Everyone took a deep breath, and the door closed. Teddy had never been in the elevator with so many people. He pushed number seven, and the elevator began to move. But a moment later the elevator stopped between the fifth and the sixth floor.

"We're not moving," said Justin, who was shoved into a back corner.

"Maybe there's another power failure," said Elizabeth. "My father got stuck in an elevator the last time."

"I know what to do," said Teddy. There was a bright red button labeled *Alarm.* Ever since he could remember he had wanted to push that button, but his parents had strictly forbidden it. Now, however, was the right moment to push it, and so Teddy did. A loud bell began to ring. It sounded like a fire drill at school. The alarm made so much noise that Teddy was sure his mother would hear it in their apartment. She would call for help.

Emily was scared and she began to cry.

"Pretend we are in a space capsule going to the moon," instructed Linda. "Let's have a countdown. Maybe by the time we reach one we will blast off."

The whole kindergarten class began to count. "Ten-nine-eight-seven-six-five-four. . . ." Even Emily was counting and not crying anymore.

Just as they were about to reach the count of three, the elevator began to move again. It stopped at the sixth floor, and the door opened. There stood Mr. Roberts with his case of tools. He was the building custodian, and he fixed things whenever they got broken.

"Class, we will get out here and walk," said Linda with relief.

"That's a good idea. The elevator is really too small to carry so many people," said Mr. Roberts, watching with an amazed expression as all the children got out of the elevator. "I've got some fixing to do."

"Aw!" groaned the children. They had enjoyed being stuck in the elevator.

There was only one more floor to walk, and the class tramped up the steps. Teddy's mother was standing at the door to greet them.

"I heard you coming all the way," she said.

"We were detained by the elevator," apologized Linda.

"Yes, thank goodness," said Mommy.

The class marched in. There weren't enough chairs, so all the children sat on the floor in the living room. Mommy passed around a box of cookies and paper cups (left over from Nora's last party). Every child got half a cup of milk, so there would be enough to go around. Only two children spilled on the rug.

They all admired Mr. Hush, the tortoise. Teddy felt proud. He wanted to do something special because he was feeling happy. Then he had an idea. He ran to his bedroom and came back holding his old Superman cape.

"This is a present for the class," he said to Linda. "You can put it in the costume box in our classroom."

"Teddy, are you sure you want to part with your cape?" asked Mommy.

"Yes," said Teddy, nodding his head. "I can still use it sometimes when I'm at school. But I'm getting too big for it."

Soon it was time to leave. "Won't Nora be surprised?" said Teddy to Mommy, as he walked out the door with his classmates.

"She certainly will. But no more than I was when you arrived."

It took as long to go downstairs as it had to come up, because Linda insisted that they walk all the way down. When they reached the street, Teddy put his hand in his pocket and discovered the kumquat that he had put there.

"Could we go back?" he asked. "I forgot to show my mother the kumquat."

"Not on your life," said Linda. "We've got to go back to school."

"Oh, well." Teddy shrugged good-naturedly. That would be another surprise for his mother and Nora in the afternoon. And wait until Nora heard that he got stuck in the elevator and pushed the red button. She had never done that!

Once again Teddy was feeling super.